D1058259

BEE THE CHANGE

The Big idea Gang

BEE THE CHANGE

By James Preller

Illustrated by Stephen Gilpin

Houghton Mifflin Harcourt

BOSTON   NEW YORK

hmhco.com

The text was set in Adobe Caslon Pro.

The Library of Congress Cataloging-in-Publication data is on file.

ISBN: 978-1-328-85770-5 hardcover
ISBN: 978-1-328-97339-9 paperback

Printed in the United States of America
DOC 10 9 8 7 6 5 4 3 2 1
4500762654

For Jim Mullen, teacher, friend

—J. P.

Table of Contents

CHAPTER 1

Top Secret!

Lizzy O'Malley opened the front door before Kym Park even reached the top step. "Give me a minute. I'm almost ready."

It was nine o'clock on a sunny Saturday morning. A good time to catch up on sleep. But not for Lizzy and Kym. They were going to meet a beekeeper.

Kym held up a finger to her father, who was parked in the driveway. *One minute*, she signaled. Kym entered the living room.

Lizzy's twin brother, Connor, was lounging on the couch. He was awake, but barely. There was still sleep in his eyes and a bowl of dry cereal on his lap.

"Hey, Connor," Kym said. "Do you want to come too?"

"Where are you going?" he asked.

"My parents' friend is a beekeeper," Kym said. "We're driving out to his farm for the day. I'm super excited."

"Bees? No, thanks," Connor said. "I don't like getting stung. Besides, I already have plans for today. I have a thing."

"A thing?"

"Yeah, Deon and I are . . . well, it's top secret," Connor said, holding up a hand. "I promised Deon I wouldn't tell a soul."

Kym stepped closer. "Come on, what's the big secret?"

"Sorry, but I've taken a solemn oath," Connor explained. "There's no way you can make me tell. Wild horses couldn't drag it out of me. Not now, not ever."

Kym shrugged. "Sure, whatever."

Lizzy hurried into the room with a backpack slung over her shoulder. "I brought a package of Oreos," she said. "I figured we might need them. You know, in case of an emergency."

"Not cool!" Connor protested, tossing a pillow in Lizzy's direction.

"Tough cookies," Lizzy said, grinning at her twin.

Kym reached for the door. "Catch you next time, Connor."

"Okay, okay," Connor said, rising from his seat. "If you're going to make a big deal out of it, Kym, I'll tell you."

"No, I'm good," Kym said.

Connor followed the two girls to the doorway. "Okay, if you absolutely have to know, Deon and I are making our own superhero comic book. It's going to be a really big deal and we're probably going to become millionaires, maybe zillionaires. It could even be a movie. I'm just saying. There. I told you. Happy now?"

"You are awesome at keeping secrets," Kym teased.

A car horn tooted. Mr. Park wasn't the kind of dad who liked to be kept waiting.

"Let's go," Kym said to Lizzy. They climbed into the back seat. Kym's parents sat up front.

Connor called after them, "Remember, don't tell anyone! It's top secret!" Connor waved good-bye and closed the door. He didn't understand why anybody would want to go visit a bunch of bees. It struck him as kind of weird. And possibly painful.

The drive to the farm took the girls into the rural countryside. The suburban houses, packed tightly together like crayons in a box, gradually fell away. They first drove on a highway, then turned onto a narrow road. The land opened up. Kym noticed more trees, more space, and, strangely, more sky. Her father pointed out a hawk soaring in the wind, wings motionless. They saw silos and barns and gray stone walls. The early April day was warm and inviting. It felt to Lizzy as if the whole world was a flower raising its petals to the sun. Kym pointed out a dozen cows standing by a barbed-wire fence. The animals chewed slowly—as if lost in thought—and with round eyes watched the car drive past.

"I love cows," Lizzy murmured. "There's so much emotion in their eyes."

"Yeah," Kym said. She knew exactly what Lizzy meant.

"I wonder what they think about?" Lizzy said.

"They do seem thoughtful," Mr. Park mused. "Philosophy, perhaps. They contemplate the meaning of life."

"Or cow pies," Kym snorted.

"We're getting close," Mrs. Park noted from the front seat. "It's good to get out into the country, isn't it?"

"It's beautiful," Lizzy agreed. "Thanks for taking us."

"It's actually not that far from where we live," Mrs. Park said. "But it feels like a million miles away."

The car slowed and Mr. Park pointed to the left. "Look, girls—wild turkeys."

"Cool," Lizzy and Kym murmured, craning their necks to see. The turkeys were dark and surprisingly large. They walked on skinny legs, pecking in the high grass.

"Benjamin Franklin argued that the turkey should be named the official bird of the United States," Mr. Park explained. "It lost out to the bald eagle."

"Good call," Kym said.

The car turned onto a dirt driveway.

"Here we are, girls. The Bee's Knees."

— CHAPTER 2 —

Ozzie

Ozzie Johnson was standing in front of a large red house when the car pulled up. He waved enthusiastically to his guests. "Greetings, Earthlings!" he called out, cackling. Ozzie scooped up a live chicken that wandered into the driveway and gently tucked it in the crook of his arm. A lively dog, black with patches of white, wove in and around Ozzie's footsteps.

After a quick hug with Kym's parents, Ozzie turned to the girls. "Welcome to my little farm. The dog's name is Yazger, and he pretty much runs the place. This lady here," he said, referring to the chicken in his right arm, "is Lulubelle. Her eggs are the best this side of the Mississippi." He

cackled again, throwing back his head, wildly entertained.

Ozzie wore jeans, a red-checked shirt, and a well-worn brown jacket with patches on the elbows. His skin was very dark, like smooth leather, and his hair and beard were tightly coiled and completely white. His eyes gleamed like stars in the night sky. The smile never left his face.

"Come inside, please," Ozzie said, flinging open the front door with an elegant bow. He pointed at Kym. "I know you are here for the bees, young lady, but first we break bread. I baked a fresh loaf this very morning. I'm sure there's homemade raspberry jam somewhere in these cupboards. Yum, delicious." He laughed again, touching his belly. "It's so nice to have visitors. I can't talk to Yazger all day long!"

The dog, Yazger, looked up at the sound of his name. He led the way into the kitchen.

After sweet tea and warm bread, Ozzie went to fetch protective outfits for the girls. Kym's parents offered to stay behind to do the dishes. They seemed relaxed and content.

"Let me get you ladies sorted out," Ozzie said. He gave Lizzy and Kym hats with veils, bright-yellow jumpsuits, and thick gloves.

"Fun," Lizzy said. "You look great, Kym." Lizzy felt nervous excitement ripple through her body like electricity. "What about you, Mr. Johnson?"

Ozzie waved a hand. "Oh, those bees don't usually bother with me. I don't make any sudden moves." He winked. "Just the same, I'll throw on a hood and veil and maybe some gloves when we get close. Come on, let's ramble."

They had walked about fifty yards when Ozzie pointed. "See it now? That's a hive box. This one's about medium-size."

"It almost looks like a dresser for a bedroom," Lizzy observed.

"Yeah, I guess you're right," Ozzie said, nodding. "A dresser filled with bees. Are you ready to take a closer look?"

"You bet," Kym said.

Lizzy, to her surprise, felt a little less sure. Between Lizzy and Kym, it was usually Lizzy who was bolder and more adventurous. But not today.

"See that blue folding chair over there?" Ozzie pointed. "I come out here to read my mystery novels. I watch the bees come and go—get a sense of the hive's activity—and commune with Mother Earth."

Ozzie chuckled over that one, eyes gleaming.

He stepped into a tidy garden shed and emerged holding a toolbox in his left hand. In his right, Ozzie carried a round metal cylinder with a tilted cone on the top. A cloud of gray-white smoke leaked out of it. "This is the beekeeper's friend," Ozzie explained. "The smoke calms the bees down. Keeps 'em mellow. I bring a smoker whenever I'm going to take a look inside. We don't want to agitate the bees."

"It looks like something the Tin Man from *The Wizard of Oz* would wear on his head," Lizzy joked.

"That's me, the wizard of Ozzie!" The old man grinned. He paused about twenty feet from the hive box. "Easy now," Ozzie said in a soft voice. "Take a look from here, ladies. What do you see?"

Kym and Lizzy noticed a number of bees moving around the hive box, arriving and departing from a narrow opening near the bottom.

"Bees," Kym whispered.

"That's a good sign," Ozzie said. "It's a warm

spring day. A healthy hive should be busy this time of year. If you look close, you'll see some of them are covered with orange pollen they picked up from the flowers."

"Oh, I see it!" Kym said.

"Pretty cool, am I right? I don't want you to be afraid of my bees," Ozzie said.

Kym nodded. "Of course."

"Honeybees have work to do. Flowers to visit. Nectar to gather. The queen has eggs to lay. They don't *want* to sting anybody. They only do it if they feel threatened. Did you know," Ozzie said, "that a honeybee dies after it stings? Do you think they *want* to die? Just leave 'em be, move slowly, and bees won't bother you. Unfortunately, today we're going to bother them a little bit— that's the peril of being a beekeeper."

Ozzie pulled the hood over his head. He stepped forward. He directed the smoke into the area of the hive. After a few minutes, Ozzie gestured for the girls to step closer. "Now let's have a look-see," he said.

Kym leaned forward.

Lizzy stepped back.

Ozzie lifted off the roof and inner cover. "Ah, the sweet stuff," he murmured.

CHAPTER 3

A Meeting with the Queen

"It's okay, my friends," Ozzie said in a soothing voice. He was talking to the honeybees. "Just checking up on you all."

He slid out a wooden frame. With a brush, the beekeeper gently pushed aside a number of bees that were crawling on it. They flew away, unharmed. "See that, ladies? Honey, golden and delicious. Amazing, isn't it? I'll add an extra frame later today to make sure the bees have room to produce more." Satisfied with his inspection, Ozzie slid the frame back into the top drawer, which he called the "honey super."

"Is the queen in there?" Kym asked.

Ozzie shook his head. "We keep the queen away from the honey. We don't want sticky eggs." Ozzie lifted the entire top box, the honey super filled with frames, and set it on the ground.

"Now let's try to locate Her Majesty the Queen," Ozzie said, his voice soft and soothing. He returned his attention to the bottom half of the hive box. Ozzie pulled out a metal screen. "See here? This is called a queen excluder. The

holes are large enough for worker bees—the ones that make the honey—but too small for the queen bee to squeeze through. Below that, in here, we have the brood supers. That's where the eggs are laid. Lot of bees in here."

Lizzie was relieved to see him once again blow smoke across the top of the box. It took a bit of muscle, prying with his tools, before Ozzie could lift out a frame from the brood super.

The frame was a crawling mass of bees.

Gross, Lizzy thought.

"Beautiful," Kym said. "So many!"

Ozzie grinned from behind the veil. "There could be as many as thirty thousand bees in a single hive, sometimes more. Come closer for a look."

Kym stepped beside Ozzie.

Lizzy stood planted on her tippy toes, leaning in. She didn't want to get too close.

"That's larvae," Ozzy explained.

"I don't understand," Lizzy said.

"A larva is an in-between stage in the bee's metamorphosis," Ozzy said, turning to look at the girls. "And before you ask, 'metamorphosis' is a big word that means change. First there's the egg, then it becomes a larva. It's immature, worm-like, no wings yet, not a bee yet." He pointed out white bits in the honeycomb pattern. "Later they will be covered over by the workers, or capped, and the larvae will transform into bees."

"Cool," Kym gushed.

QUEEN LAYS AN EGG

EGG HATCHES

LARVA APPEARS

PUPA STAGE BEGINS

ADULT BEE JOINS THE COLONY

"It is pure magic on this earth," Ozzy said. "I love it."

Frame by frame, Ozzie inspected the hive. "Ah, here she is," he said, giving a little bow. "Good day, Your Majesty." He turned to Lizzy. "It's okay, sweetie. Trust me. Here, you can hold it."

Ozzie held out the frame, boiling with bees, for Lizzy to take.

Lizzy shook her head. "No . . . I'm good," she answered in a halting voice.

"I'll hold it," Kym offered. For some reason, Kym wasn't afraid of a thing. Perhaps she was too fascinated to feel any fear.

Ozzie pointed. "There she is, the queen. See that little crown she wears on her head?" Ozzie laughed, winking at his guests. "The queen is bigger than the others."

Finished at last, Ozzie reconstructed the hive. He reinserted each frame. He carefully stacked the supers on top of each other. "Let's go find your folks," Ozzie said, leading the girls back to the farmhouse.

Lizzy pondered as they walked. "Mr. Johnson, I have a question."

"Fire away," he replied. "But call me Ozzie, please."

"Okay . . . Ozzie." Lizzy bit her lip, not wishing to offend her host. "I mean, why bees?"

"I love bees!" Ozzie gushed.

"Yes, but why? I don't get it," Lizzy said.

"Honeybees are important," Ozzie said. "They are pollinators. Without honeybees, we'd have no—"

"Honey?" Kym interjected.

"Ha, that's right," Ozzie replied. "But that's just the start. Bees have a big impact on the food chain. They are important to many different plants, fruits, and vegetables. Without honeybees, we wouldn't have lilacs or squash, pumpkins or sunflowers. The list goes on forever. Crops like almonds, cherries, apples, oranges, alfalfa, and

soybeans all depend on the work of bees. Without bees, the world would be a much poorer place. Our food and bees are interdependent."

"Inter-what?" Lizzy asked.

"Dependent," Ozzie replied. "It means they need each other to survive. In nature, everything connects. Without bees acting as pollinators, many plants would die. And the bees would starve without plants!"

"Is that why you are a beekeeper?" Lizzy wondered.

"More or less," Ozzie replied. "About the year 2007, many beekeepers began to notice a terrible thing—their honeybees were disappearing. Millions and millions abandoned their hives. Gone, vanished. They just flew away and never came back. They died, of course. It was a great mystery why this was happening. Scientists studied the problem and called it colony collapse disorder. In order to survive, honeybees needed our help— so I decided it was time to do something. That's when I got my first hive. I've been keeping bees ever since!"

"How many hives have you got?" Kym asked.

"Twelve," Ozzie said with a delighted cackle. "I'm hooked on bees, ladies. It's like a fever. And the only cure is . . . more bees!"

His laughter filled the meadow and filtered through the open windows of the farmhouse, where Kym's parents patiently waited.

They sipped honey tea.

— CHAPTER 4 —

Slug Man

Meanwhile, in a secret hideout in a galaxy far, far away (well, okay, in Deon Gibson's basement), two boys sat down with an amazing plan. Connor O'Malley and Deon Gibson decided to create the most terrific, most awesome, most really-really-super-cool superhero comic book of all time.

They were ready to rock and roll.

They had plenty of paper. Pens and markers. Drinks and snacks. Everything two artists could possibly need.

Except . . .

"We're missing one thing," Deon concluded.

"Yeah, what's that?" Connor asked. He tossed a pretzel nugget into the air and tried to catch it in his mouth. The nugget bounced off his fore-head and onto the rug.

Deon smirked. "You are really bad at that, you know."

There were already half a dozen pretzel nug-gets on the floor.

"Don't worry, I'll clean it up before we go," Connor said.

"That's right, you will," Deon said. "But first, read out loud what we've got so far."

Connor picked up his notebook.

He coughed and began to read. "Deep in his remote hideout."

Connor stopped reading. He set down the notebook and looked at Deon.

Deon looked back. "That's it?"

"So far," Connor said.

"It's not bad," Deon said.

"Not bad is pretty good," Connor reasoned. "Maybe we should take a break."

Deon shook his head. "We can do this, Connor. We've just got to work at it. Look at the popularity of superhero movies—all making huge money. *Iron Man, Thor, Batman, Ant-Man, Black Panther.* We need to come up with our own action hero."

Connor leaned forward. He brought his elbows to his knees, tucked his fists under his chin. "Let's think of different animals. We can't use bats and spiders or ants, obviously."

Deon nodded. "Already taken. What about . . . Gorilla Man?"

"Too much like Tarzan," Connor replied. "The rhino?"

"Nah," Deon replied. "I think that's one of the bad guys in the Spider-Man comics. He crashes into walls or something."

"Rats," Connor groaned.

"Rat Man?" Deon said, eyebrows raised.

"Sounds too much like Batman," Connor said. He tossed another pretzel into the air, lunged to his left, and the nugget hit him in the eye. It seemed to give him an idea.

"I've got it!" Connor exclaimed. "How about . . . SLUG MAN!"

Deon's eyebrows arched. "What's his superpower?"

"He slimes people!" Connor said.

Inspired, Deon snatched up his markers. He drew a crude picture of a bad guy trapped in green ooze. Deon added a word balloon: "DRATS! I've been oozed by green crud!"

"Great writing!" Connor said, patting Deon on the back. "What about, like, I don't know, if you added a big long trail of slime?"

"Genius," Deon said, giggling. He reached for a green marker.

"What other powers should he have?" Connor wondered. He snapped his fingers. "Hey, slugs have those weird antennae, don't they? Maybe he can hear stuff that's far away?"

"Yeah," Deon said. "He, like, senses vibrations in the galaxy."

That's how the two friends spent the next hour, laughing, snickering, drawing, and writing. But after a while, their comic book lost steam. Slugs were kind of boring, they eventually decided, even ones with superpowers.

"It kind of looks like a giant booger," Deon conceded.

"Yeah, I see what you mean," Connor said, frowning. "Maybe a slug with superpowers is not what America needs right now. These million-dollar ideas are tough."

Oh well. At least the two friends had a good time.

Connor never did catch a pretzel nugget in his mouth.

— CHAPTER 5 —

Inspired

Miss Isadora Bliss Zipsokowski—known as Miss Zips—stood outside room 312, greeting her students as they entered the classroom.

"Morning . . . morning . . . how ya doing?" she'd say, smiling at each and every student who came down the hall. Even the grumpy ones. Miss Zips was long and lanky and had a small, sharp nose and large feet.

Her students loved her. They knew that even though Miss Zips could be tough, she cared about them. No matter what, no matter who. She even seemed to enjoy Otis Smick, who drove other teachers crazy. It wasn't Otis's fault. He didn't mean to be a headache. It just came naturally.

"Good morning, Kym," Miss Zips said. "How was your weekend?"

Kym stopped in her tracks to look up, and up, at her very tall teacher. "Inspiring," Kym said with a big smile. "Two thumbs up!"

"Inspiring? I like the sound of that," Miss Zips said.

"Lizzy and I visited a farm with my parents,"

Kym continued. "I had the best time ever. And, oh, we met a queen."

"A queen!" Miss Zips exclaimed, bringing her hands to her face. "You'll have to tell us about it later in class. But we better duck inside. It's almost time for the bell."

After Kym got herself sorted out at the cubbies, she sat down at her table. Miss Zips called it a table, but really it was just four desks smooshed together. Each month Miss Zips had the students change seats. This month wasn't a perfect arrangement from Kym's point of view. The other kids at her table were Connor (he was nice), Suri Brewster (a little too perfect), and Otis Smick (ugh).

Otis wasn't bad, truthfully. He meant well. Kym had to resist the urge to brush his hair, though. What a mess!

"Hey, Kym," Connor said. "I heard you guys had fun at the farm."

"Yeah, it was great," Kym replied.

"HI, KYM! WANT TO SWAP LUNCHES TODAY? I HAVE LIVERWURST!" Otis said. (His voice was always a half shout.)

"Morning, Otis," Kym replied without enthusiasm. She ignored his question. Kym Park was not the type of person who would swap lunches with Otis Smick. Not happening. No way. So she busied herself by organizing her folders and lining up her pencils. "Oh, Connor, I forgot to ask." Kym lowered her voice to a whisper. "How did it go with your top-secret project?"

Connor shrugged. "Our superhero turned out to be a super dud."

"Oh?"

"Slug Man," Connor said.

Kym laughed. "Seriously?"

"It seemed like a good idea at the time," Connor said with a grin. "Making up a superhero is harder than I realized. All the good animals are already taken—bats and panthers and spiders and stuff."

"What about bees?" Kym asked.

Connor shrugged. "There's a wasp hero, but I don't think there are any bees."

"There should be!" Kym suggested. "Honey-bees are amazing."

"Bees are scary," Suri interjected. "I'm not a fan."

Poor bees, Kym thought. *So misunderstood.*

Connor pondered for a moment. "Bee Man," he said in a deep voice. He liked the sound of it.

"BEE MAN!" Otis Smick shouted. "HIS STINGER KILLS THE WORLD! BOO-YAH!" Otis pumped both fists in the air.

Kym sighed.

"Or Bee Woman," Kym pointed out. "Doesn't have to be a man to be a hero. Besides, only fe-male bees have stingers. The males are called drones. Pretty useless, if you ask me."

"Darn," Otis Smick muttered. He didn't shout, for a change.

CHAPTER 6

The Beginning of an Idea

The playground behind Clay Elementary covered a sprawling area of open field and shady slopes, featuring balance beams and climbing walls, swing sets and monkey bars, and, closest to the building, a basketball court. On this April afternoon, students ran around in T-shirts and shorts. They shouted and laughed, free from winter at last. A boisterous group jostled on the basketball court, Padma Bitar and a few friends laughed by the buddy bench, and Bobby Mumford quietly organized a row of small stones.

Four friends—Connor, Deon, Lizzy, and

Kym—gathered in conversation. They could feel it: *the beginning of an idea.*

A big idea.

Kym talked the most. And when she was done, Deon nodded. "Let's go talk to the Zipster."

"Now?" Kym said. "It's recess."

Deon didn't even glance back to answer. He just headed into the school. His friends followed. They ran into Miss Zips in the hallway.

"What's up?" she asked. The teacher checked her wristwatch. "You guys still have ten minutes of recess, then Mr. Sanders will be bringing you to music."

"We were hoping . . ." Kym's voice faltered.

Miss Zips carried a thick stack of student journals in her right arm. She shifted to rest them on her hip.

"We wanted to talk to you about something," Lizzy spoke up.

Miss Zips glanced down the hall in the direction of the teacher's lounge. She began, "I had hoped to use this time to grade . . ." Then Miss Zips looked down at Kym, who stared back with imploring eyes. Miss Zips shifted the heavy books to her other arm. And in that time she made a decision. "Sure," she said, smiling. "I can always read essays at home. Let's talk in the classroom—as long as you don't mind if I eat my lunch while we do it."

Once settled at her desk, Miss Zips popped open a plastic container of mixed fruit. "Is this about the honeybees?" she asked.

Lizzy was surprised. "How'd you know?"

"Oh, someone was buzzing in my ear earlier today," Miss Zips said, shifting her eyes to Kym.

"Yeah, we're into bees now, I guess," Connor said. He didn't seem convinced.

"Forgive me, I'm still not clear," Miss Zips said. "What is it that you want?"

Kym looked at Connor, Deon, and Lizzy. They all seemed to be waiting for her to take the lead. "We want people to learn more about honeybees," Kym said, her voice a bit firmer than usual. "We want people to like them. We want" —she paused—"to make a difference."

Miss Zips put down her spoon. She wiped her mouth with a napkin. "Wow," she said, bringing a hand to her heart. "That was amazing, Kym. You just wowed me. How can I help?"

Kym talked about the importance of honey-

bees. And about colony collapse disorder. She even pointed out the fruit that Miss Zips was eating. "Without bees, it would be very hard to find blueberries, apples, and oranges."

"Yes, I agree with you. It seems to me that you want to convince your classmates that bees are important," Miss Zips said.

"Not just classmates," Deon said, holding open his arms wide. "The entire galaxy."

Miss Zips laughed. "Oh, Deon. You do think big. Let's start small and see how it goes."

"What's bigger?" Deon wondered. "A galaxy, a solar system, or the universe?"

"Your mouth," Connor joked.

"I heard that!" Deon said. He tilted his head back and opened his mouth wide like a baby bird in a nest.

"Focus, Deon," Lizzy said. "We're talking about bees, please."

"Deon's right," Connor interjected. "Why stop with just our classmates? Why not teach the whole school? I mean, if you think it would be okay, Miss Zips."

"The whole school," Miss Zips echoed. "Well, you can certainly try to convince all of Clay Elementary that honeybees are wonderful. That's fine and good. But let's think deeper. What are you hoping to achieve?"

The students looked at their teacher with blank faces.

Miss Zips prodded: "Ask yourselves, *What do you want your fellow students to do?*"

Lizzy shrugged.

"We haven't gotten that far," Kym admitted.

"Do you want to persuade them to become beekeepers?" Miss Zips asked.

Connor raised two hands. "Yeah, not happening. Bees are cool and everything, but that's a hard no."

"We want them to care," Kym offered.

"Care? Okay, fine. But what *action* do you want them to take? I think you need to give this more thought. Do some research. Try to find specific things that students can *do* to help the honeybees."

Back at their desks, waiting for Mr. Sanders to bring them to music class, Deon shook his head. "Unbelievable," he groaned.

"What?" asked Connor.

"Typical Zipster," Deon whispered. "Every time we ask her for help, she gives us homework."

"We'll meet in the library after school," Kym announced. She reached into her desk, pulled out a book, and started reading. It was about honeybees.

— CHAPTER 7 —

The Return of Otis Smick

"Listen to this, it's so cool," Connor said as he read from a library book. "'Bees have five eyes and'—get this!—'worker bees can make wax from their abdomen.'"

"Wax! That's crazy," Deon gushed. And after a pause, he asked, "Um, what's an abdomen?"

"It's a stomach, I think," Connor said. "Like abs, you know?"

"Here's a good one," Deon said. "Bees were alive in the time of the dinosaurs. That's seriously old. They must be tough. It's weird they are disappearing now. I wonder why."

Connor looked up. "Here comes Kym and Lizzy." He scooted over to make room. The four friends sat in their favorite spot at the town library—a comfy horseshoe-shaped couch tucked in the corner of the building. Books and art supplies were scattered on the table, on the floor, everywhere.

"I hereby call to order today's meeting of the Big Idea Gang," Lizzy announced. "BIG for short. What have you got so far?"

"We've been gathering bee facts," Connor said. "And I have to admit it. A bee will definitely make a good comic-book hero."

Kym leafed through Deon's scribbled drawings on the table. "That's it? You guys have spent all your time writing a comic book?"

"We were inspired," Deon explained.

"We're here to save the bees," Kym protested. "Not draw pictures."

"Hey, leave us alone. Bee Girl is super cool—she has a sack of venom *and* a stinger," Connor

said. "She can flap her wings two hundred and thirty times per second. That's nuts. If we want people to like bees, a comic book might help."

"My brother actually has a point," Lizzy admitted.

"I do?" Connor said.

"WHAT'S UP, DUDES!" a loud voice interrupted.

It was Otis Smick.

"IT'S CRAZY YOU DUDES ARE HERE! GUESS WHAT? I AM TOO!" he barked.

"Otis, what are *you* doing in the library?" Kym asked.

"THE 3-D PRINTER," Otis said. "THERE'S A MAKER ROOM IN THE BACK."

Kym smiled weakly. She waited for Otis to leave.

Otis didn't move.

He stood gaping at them. Mouth open. Mop of hair in his face.

"WHAT ARE YOU DUDES DOING?" he asked.

"Nothing," Kym replied.

But Connor said, "We're trying to save the world one bee at a time. Want to help?"

Kym shot Connor the evil eye. But before she could utter a word in protest, Otis howled, "AWESOMESAUCE!" He plopped himself on the couch.

Even Kym had to laugh at Otis Smick's enthusiasm. He was like a Labrador retriever chasing after a tennis ball.

Lizzy had a suggestion. "Maybe we could make a list of fun facts about honeybees. Connor and Deon have already gotten off to a great start."

"LISTS ARE AWESOMESAUCE!" commented Otis, nodding happily.

"Er, yes," Lizzy said, taking Kym by the hand. "Meanwhile, I need to borrow Kym for a minute."

"CAN I COME?" Otis bounded forward.

Kym's left eyelid twitched.

Lizzy smiled. "Thanks, Otis. But it's better if

you help the guys. Kym and I need to speak in private."

"COOL! SURE!" Otis replied. "THAT'S AWE—"

"Awesomesauce," Lizzy said. "Yeah, we know."

Lizzy steered Kym toward the front doors. Suddenly, she stopped. "Otis?" she asked, turning back to look at the mop-haired boy.

"YEAH?"

"I was wondering. Do you *like* bees?" Lizzy asked.

Otis shrugged. "Sure, I guess."

"How would you help them?" Lizzy asked. "I mean, if you wanted to help them? What would you do?"

Otis raised his palms to the sky. "WHO KNOWS?"

Lizzy nodded, satisfied. "Thanks, Otis. You've been very helpful."

"I HAVE?" Otis seemed surprised. He wasn't called "helpful" very often.

"Oh, yes," Lizzy said. She gave Kym a gentle

tug and again the two girls headed to the doors that led outside.

"Thank you," Kym whispered as the girls walked away. "Otis drives me bananas."

"I think he likes you," Lizzy said, teasing.

"Ugh, oh no," Kym groaned.

"He's sweet," Lizzy said.

"He's a caveman," Kym muttered.

"Perhaps," Lizzy agreed. "But he's an awfully sweet caveman."

— CHAPTER 8 —

Bee the Change

"Let's talk outside. It's a gorgeous day," Lizzy said.

The girls stepped outside and found a shady spot on the grass. Behind them, a man in blue overalls dragged an iron rake through the flower beds. A woman in a straw hat knelt on her hands and knees, digging in the dirt.

"You know what we need, don't you?" Lizzy asked.

Kym said she didn't know.

"Ozzie," Lizzy replied.

"What do you mean?" Kym asked.

"Think about it, Kym. He could come to our school and give a talk about honeybees," Lizzy suggested. "That would get everyone excited."

"I don't know," Kym demurred. When it came to asking for things, Kym wasn't confident. She wasn't afraid of bees, but speaking up, for Kym, was a lot scarier.

"What are you worried about?" Lizzy asked. "It's Ozzie! He's friends with your parents. He loves bees! I bet he'd be happy to visit our school. It can't hurt to ask."

"We can't assume Principal Tuxbury will let us," Kym countered.

Lizzy waved a hand. "Of course he will. Mr. Tuxbury loves that stuff, you know that. He's always bringing in experts."

Scritch-scratch, scritch-scratch. The gardener raked through the dirt, stirring it up after winter's long sleep.

"You know what? I wish we could have a hive at school," Kym said.

"I doubt Principal Tuxbury would go for that," Lizzy said.

"I guess you're right," Kym said. The girls

lapsed into silence. Kym plucked a yellow dandelion from the grass and turned it in her fingers. "Hey, Lizzy," she said. "Why were you asking Otis if he liked bees?"

Lizzy leaned back on her hands. "The important question I asked was what he'd do if he wanted to help them," she said.

Kym laughed. "Yeah, and he had no idea!"

"I bet that's true for most people," Lizzy said. "I think that's what Miss Zips was trying to tell us. We have to show people what they can do. We need them to participate."

Kym nodded. "Okay, first we get them to appreciate honeybees. Then we show them how they can help. Is that it?"

"Exactamundo," Lizzy said. "Let's activate!"

Again the girls lapsed into a thoughtful silence. A cardinal landed near the garden. Kym suddenly bolted into an upright position. She clapped her hands. "I've got it! I just figured it out, Lizzy—I know how we can get kids to help—and it's a beautiful idea."

* * *

Back inside the library, the boys were busy brainstorming. They had written out fun facts about bees on separate pieces of paper. But they weren't satisfied.

"Something's missing." Deon frowned. "It's just, I don't know, boring. Facts aren't enough."

"You remember when we did persuasive writing in class?" Connor said. "Miss Zips told us we needed to grab people's attention. We can't be dull. Nobody will pay attention."

"What if we had a snazzy slogan?" Deon said. He snapped his fingers. "I've got it!" Deon grabbed a marker and wrote these words in big, bold letters:

BEE THE CHANGE!

Deon colored the letters in yellow and black stripes.

"Sweet, I like it," Connor said.

"HEY GUYS! I HAVE AN IDEA TOO!" Otis Smick said.

Connor and Deon turned to Otis, surprised. As far as they could tell, Otis Smick had not had an idea for the entire school year. It was already April.

"Okaaay?" Deon said.

"WE SHOULD MAKE A GIGANTIC HONEYBEE!"

Deon raised an eyebrow. "Hmmmm. That's actually not terrible, Otis."

"WE'LL USE WIRE AND PAPIER-MÂCHÉ! IT WILL BE BIGGER THAN THE ENTIRE SCHOOL! WE'LL FILL IT WITH BALLOONS AND IT WILL FLOAT LIKE A HUNDRED-THOUSAND FEET IN THE AIR!" Otis continued.

"Easy, Otis," Connor said. "You have a good idea there. Let's not go crazy."

"Maybe a bee mobile?" Deon suggested. "Like, I don't know, colorful bees hanging from the ceiling in the school lobby."

The boys sat in silence, all three with a chin resting on their hands, imagining the scene: Bees and bee facts filling the school entranceway. And a big banner that read BEE THE CHANGE.

Otis Smick beamed with pure joy.

"AWESOMESAUCE!" he said.

CHAPTER 9

Busy and Buzzing

Over the next two weeks, the Big Idea Gang was as busy as—you guessed it—bees. There was so much to be done. Fortunately, once they got the ball rolling, a lot of folks helped out.

"That's the thing with good ideas," Miss Zips said. "They're contagious."

"Like the flu," Connor said.

He sneezed.

"Yes," Miss Zips said, "like the flu." She reached for the Purell wipes.

* * *

For starters, Kym had to call Ozzie to ask if he'd be willing to visit the school.

Ozzie loved her big idea.

"Can I bring my bees?" Ozzie asked.

Kym wasn't so sure about that.

"What about Lulubelle?" he wondered, thinking of his favorite chicken.

"Possibly," Kym replied.

"I'll do a PowerPoint," Ozzie decided. "Thanks for asking. It'll be a blast!"

"Thank you, Ozzie. Remember, we don't have approval yet," Kym cautioned. "We just wanted to check to see if you were willing to come."

"Say the word and I'll be there, and I'll bring Lulubelle!" the beekeeper said. And once again he cackled, for no reason other than he was a man who liked the sound of his own laughter.

Next, Kym and Lizzy met with Principal Tuxbury. He thought having a beekeeper visit

the school was a terrific idea. "I'm all for it!" he exclaimed. "Get me his number and I'll call Mr. Ozzie Johnson today. We need to make this official."

* * *

Connor and Deon (and, yes, Otis too) took charge of decorating the front lobby. They researched and neatly wrote out seventeen fascinating facts about honeybees. Even the art teacher, Mrs. O'Keefe, got into it. She helped the younger students make toilet-paper-roll honeybees. They taped yellow construction paper around toilet paper rolls, cut out black stripes, and glued on googly eyes and wings. Hanging from each bee was a fun fact.

"Pretty darn cute," Principal Tuxbury observed. "Educational, too!"

* * *

Otis was in charge of hanging the giant banner in the lobby. (Maybe that wasn't the best idea.)

"Careful up there, Otis," Principal Tuxbury said. He pulled nervously on his lower lip. "I'm not entirely comfortable with you standing on that wobbly table."

Fortunately the school custodian, Janet, lent Otis a helping hand.

"Our visiting beekeeper, Mr. Johnson, will be

very pleased with our welcome when he arrives tomorrow. Just be careful not to break anything."

* * *

Finally, it was time to enact Kym's beautiful big idea.

Miss Zips listened intently. "You'll have to speak with Nurse Baez, she's the green thumb around here."

"Green thumb?" Kym repeated.

"Ms. Baez loves gardening," Miss Zips said. "She's the one who started our school garden several years back. In fact, she does most of the work by herself. I'm sure she'd love to get some help to make it bigger and better."

— CHAPTER 10 —

Bee Friendly

Ms. Yolanda Baez was an energetic, lively woman who had been school nurse for many years. She was a fitness buff and an avid runner—there was even a framed photo on the office wall of her crossing the finish line at the Boston Marathon. She looked tired, but triumphant. Her greatest passion was nature. Ms. Baez enjoyed hiking, kayaking, biking, swimming, anything that brought her outdoors.

Years ago she took it upon herself to create a garden behind the school. The PTA supported her efforts with a small donation, but it was Ms. Baez who provided the muscle. It was a small garden, but a happy sight at Clay Elementary. She grew an assortment of herbs and vegetables

—kale and carrots, cucumbers and tomatoes, that sort of thing. Plants that could be eaten. No flowers.

Kym entered the nurse's office.

Ms. Baez looked up through a pair of fashionably oversize round glasses. Banana earrings dangled from her perfect ears.

There was a boy lying face-up on a cot. He had a cool towel over his eyes and forehead. Kym knew it was Milo Pitts, who had been complaining earlier in the day of a bellyache. Kym figured he was faking it. That was how Milo rolled. He liked attention.

"Are you feeling unwell?" Ms. Baez asked Kym.

"No, I'm fine," Kym said. "I wanted to . . . um." She faltered, not sure of the words. Ms. Baez's warm smile gave her courage.

Ms. Baez gestured to a low stool. "Have a seat, please."

Kym sat.

Milo groaned.

Ms. Baez glanced in his direction. The flicker of a frown crossed her face.

"I wanted to talk to you about your garden," Kym said, gathering her courage.

"Oh, it's not *my* garden," Ms. Baez said. "It's the school's. It's yours, actually."

Kym was surprised. "Mine?"

"I'm just the gardener," Ms. Baez said. She scrunched her nose and winked. "I work cheap."

Kym laughed. She told Ms. Baez about the honeybees. "Honeybees are super important," Kym said. Ms. Baez listened patiently while Kym explained that without plants that produced nectar and pollen, bees wouldn't have food to live. "And without bees visiting the flowers to collect nectar, many plants wouldn't be able to reproduce."

"Yes, certainly," Ms. Baez said. "I'm aware of the importance of bees. It's a partnership."

"Yes!" Kym said, brightening. "A partnership between plants and bees that helps people. It gives us healthy food to eat. Like almonds, raspberries, watermelons, blueberries, and so much more."

"Bees have had a tough time lately," Ms. Baez said.

"You know about that?" Kym asked.

Ms. Baez smiled. "I try to keep up."

Kym told Ms. Baez her idea for a bee-friendly garden.

"Now I feel silly," Ms. Baez confessed. "I've planted that garden for years, but I never once looked at it from the point of view of a honeybee. Thank you, Kym. Your idea for the garden is wonderful."

"Do you think it's too late in the season?" Kym asked. "I'm not a"—she paused, trying to remember the words—"green thumb."

Ms. Baez glanced out the window. It had rained earlier that day, but now the sun fought through the clouds. The grass glistened. "No," the nurse said. "I think we'll be okay, if we plant soon. Are you going to help me?"

"Of course!" Kym said. "Not just me. My friends, too. I know lots of people who'll help."

Ms. Baez checked her calendar, thumbing through her phone. "How about . . . hmmm . . . not this Saturday . . . but the one after that?"

"Perfect timing," Kym replied. "That's the weekend after Mr. Johnson visits the school. He can even announce our plans for the garden at the end of his presentation."

"Good thinking." Ms. Baez grinned. "Everyone will be inspired! We'll get more volunteers that way."

And in that moment it felt to Kym as if her heart had suddenly, unexpectedly opened like the petals of a flower.

— CHAPTER 11 —

Seeds, Please

Kym and Lizzy stared at the rack of flower seeds at the hardware store. "It's a little intimidating," Kym said. "So many choices."

"I made a list," Lizzy said, pulling a ragged piece of paper from her pocket. "We know that bees are attracted to flowers with bright colors, especially purple and yellow."

Kym reached for a package of sunflowers. "Is one pack enough?"

"Ooooh, I love sunflowers! They grow so tall. Imagine an entire garden of sunflowers! It would make the bees so happy!" Lizzy reached for a second package.

"What else is on the list?" Kym asked.

Lizzy read the names. "Let's see, hollyhock, buttercup, snowdrop, zinnia . . ."

"You guys ready?" Connor appeared at their side.

"Where were you?" Lizzy asked.

"Dad and I were looking at power tools. It was pretty cool," he said. "I wanted a power saw, but Dad said no."

"Let's go," Kym said. "We don't want to be late."

* * *

A small crowd of students, and several teachers, met at the garden behind the school. Ozzie's visit had been a big success. He inspired the entire school. Kids were getting excited about helping the bees. Many volunteers brought their own small shovels and rakes. Some had gloves. They all looked eager to work. Even Miss Zips. Not bad for a drizzly Saturday.

"My goodness," Ms. Baez said. She whistled under her Clay Elementary Dragons baseball hat. "Thanks, everyone. I never got this much interest in the garden before."

"You know what they say. Many hands make light work," said Principal Tuxbury.

"What's that mean?" Deon asked.

"It means if we all work together—" the principal began.

"—then the job gets easier!" Ms. Baez said. "Let's start planting."

After a while, Deon leaned back on his heels. He looked across the field. "I wish Bee Girl was here to see this," he lamented. "She would have been proud."

"Right," Connor agreed.

"Do you think it's enough?" Kym wondered. "Planting flowers?"

Miss Zips stood up. She rubbed her nose with the back of her gardening glove. "I don't think we can *ever* do enough," she said. "But I believe we're making a difference."

"A small one," Kym said.

"You have to start somewhere. But it doesn't have to end here," Miss Zips said.

"That's right," Lizzy chimed in. "This is just the bee-ginning."

"You gotta bee-lieve!" Connor exclaimed.

"Corny," Kym said with a laugh.

"Yo, look," Deon said. He pointed at a bee that hovered, for a moment, over a nearby yellow dandelion.

He turned to Connor. "Don't worry, Con. Just stay nice and quiet, and that bee won't bother us."

"I know that," Connor said.

But Connor kept an eye on that bee all the while.

Until it flew away. Bee-cause, after all, that bee had an important job to do.

AMAZING, BEE-AUTIFUL BEE FACTS

Brought to you by . . . Connor and Deon!

- Honey is the only food made by insects that we can eat!

- Male honeybees are called drones.

- Female honeybees are called workers —and they are the only ones with stingers!

- A honeybee dies after it stings, so it won't sting unless it feels threatened.

- What's the buzz? A honeybee's wings beat more than 230 times per second. That's what makes the buzzy bee buzz!

- Each hive has one queen, and she has one job — to lay about 2,000 eggs a day!

- In parts of China, there are so few bees left that people pollinate fruit trees by hand! Boooooring!

- Some people think dandelions are just weeds, but the flowers are good for bees! Let 'em grow!

- Bees can't see the color red! They are most attracted to yellow, blue, purple, and white flowers.

- Honeybees produce wax from their abdomen. Humans use this wax to make all sorts of stuff—candles, cosmetics, even surfboard wax.

- One honeybee makes only one-twelfth of a teaspoon of honey in her life.

- A honeybee flies about 15 miles per hour. Zoom*!*

- In 1851, some dude named Lorenzo Langstroth designed the modern beehive that beekeepers still use today*!*

- Bees were around during the time of dinosaurs*!*

Next time you eat an apple or see a flower, thank a bee!

"You're Welcome!"

AND LASTLY . . .
THIS IS NOT A FACT, BUT . . .
Bees are the superheroes of the insect world!

Miss Zips's "Wow Me" Tips

So you want to make a difference? That's great! There are so many ways that you can make a difference in your school, your community, and even the world! But making things better means making changes, and you'll need to convince people that those changes are worth making.

What's the big idea?

Presenting an argument is not about being the loudest, or the funniest, or even the smartest. As I tell my students all the time, it's about making a claim and supporting that claim with evidence.

What do you need to convince your audience of? A claim often starts with a big idea. An idea is "big" if it is something you feel excited or passionate about. If you don't feel strongly, how can you convince anyone else to agree with you?

Kym had the big idea for a bee-friendly garden at Clay Elementary. To turn that idea into a claim, the BIG needed to be specific, direct, and make one main point: honeybees are essential to our environment and Clay Elementary should do something to help them. There is no question about what they are arguing!

Now what? Support that claim!

Supporting your claim means trying to prove it. Think about it this way: if you simply made a claim and stopped there, your audience would be left wondering, WHY? So you have to answer that question for them. You have to give your audience reasons to be persuaded, and back those reasons up with evidence such as facts and details.

It's always good to start by asking yourself some questions. For example:

- **Why are honeybees important?**

- **Why should we care that the honeybees are disappearing?**

- **What actions can the BIG take to teach others about honeybees?**

- **What do they want the other students to do about the disappearing bees?**

- **What are possible obstacles to a bee-friendly garden, and how can I argue against them?**

Being able to answer these kinds of questions will give you the reasons for your argument and help you come up with the facts and details you need to support your claim.

Let's look at Kym's argument. What support does she offer to convince Clay Elementary to help save the honeybees?

REASON: Bees are an important part of the food chain, helping fruits and vegetables grow.

EVIDENCE: Without bees acting as pollinators, many plants would die.

REASON: Bees need our help to survive.

EVIDENCE: Scientists have observed the mysterious disappearance of bees called colony collapse disorder.

REASON: A bee-friendly garden is an easy way for the students at Clay Elementary to take a first step toward helping the bees.

EVIDENCE: The school already has a small garden that the students can expand, and Kym and Lizzy can pick out bee-friendly flowers for volunteers to plant and take care of.

Wrap it up!

Now that you've made your claim and supported it with reasons and evidence, it's time to wrap everything up in the conclusion of your argument. This is your last chance to get your audience to agree with your point of view—make the most of it! In your conclusion, you can restate your claim, tie up any loose ends, and make a call to action if needed. A call to action asks your audience to believe something or do something. The BIG creates a slogan: "Bee the change!" This is a call to action because they are asking the school to support a bee-friendly garden at Clay Elementary.

Put it all together!

What we've just gone over are the basic elements of a strong argument. This is a good format to follow for your next persuasive speech, writing assignment, or anytime you want to be convincing. Now you have all the tools you need to take that first step toward making a difference.

So what's *your* big idea? Better get to work— you've got a lot of convincing to do, and I want you to wow me!